HOW TO BE A VIKING

By

Cressida Cowell

Little, Brown and Company

New York Boston

The Viking who was Seasick

Cressida Cowell

2.

Hiccup's father was Stoick the Vast.

Long ago, in a fierce and frosty land, there lived a small, lonely Viking, and his name was Hiccup.

Dear Readers and Heroes-in-training,

This was where it all began.

Sixteen years ago, I drew a picture of a little Viking called Hiccup in my sketchbook. On the opposite side of the page, I drew a picture of Hiccup's father, Chief Stoick the Vast. The story was easy to write because it was all about me, and my relationship with my own father.

I was a small, imaginative, anxious child. My father was a dashing, adventurous, ever-so-slightly-pleased-with-himself hero. He never seemed to be afraid of anything.

Who would have thought that this little picture book would have been the beginning of the twelve-book How to Train Your Dragon *fiction series? That there would be a movie made by DreamWorks, a television series, a live arena show, all based on this one little idea?*

But this was where it all began, with just me and my father. Because to a child, their father is always a hero.

Happy reading, and good luck with the hero work.

Love,

Cressida Cowell

Long ago, in a fierce and frosty land, there lived a small and lonely Viking, and his name was Hiccup.

Vikings were enormous roaring
burglars with bristling
mustaches who sailed all over
the world and took whatever
they wanted.

Hiccup was tiny and
thoughtful and polite.

The other Viking children
wouldn't let him join in their rough Viking games.

Hiccup was frightened of spiders. He was frightened of
thunder. He was frightened of sudden loud noises.

BANG!

But, most of all, he was frightened of going to sea for
the very first time . . . next Tuesday.
Hiccup wasn't sure he was a Viking at all.

Hiccup's father was

Stoick the Vast.

Wherever Stoick walked, the ground trembled, flowers wilted, and bunnies fainted. He hadn't brushed his beard in thirty years.

"Only girlie

brush their beards!"

boomed Stoick the Vast.

"Girlies don't have beards," Hiccup pointed out,
but no one listened to him.

And when Hiccup told his father he was frightened of
going to sea, Stoick laughed his enormous Viking laugh
until salty tears ran down to his enormous hairy feet.

"You can't be frightened, little Hiccup.

Vikings don't get frightened."

And he sang the Viking Song:

I have blacked the 1,000 eyes
of 1,000 angry GALES,
Watch me knock the cockles off
The biggest bluest WHALES,
I have given walrus nightmares
Who thought that they were STRONG,

I marooned a huge typho-o-o-on
On an island off Hong KONG.

O ancient prawny greenness,
The never-ending SEA,
Mess with squirmy jellyfish,
But DO NOT MESS WITH ME!

He patted Hiccup on the head and went off to do
three hundred push-ups before breakfast.
Oo-er, thought Hiccup. *It all sounds very dangerous.*

So Hiccup went to see the oldest Viking of all, Old Wrinkly
himself, whose barnacled beard fell down to his toes.
"Your Saltiness," he whispered (for Hiccup had beautiful
manners), "do Vikings ever get frightened?"

"Little grandson," wheezed Old Wrinkly, and his breath was like being kissed by mackerel, "I've been wondering about the answer to that question myself. The sea is full of trials and terrors. But it is also full of marvels and miracles. Go to sea, and you can tell me if Vikings ever get frightened."

So, at a quarter to nine on a breezy Tuesday . . .

. . . Hiccup went to sea for the very first time.

At half past nine, Hiccup
was wishing he hadn't
eaten those two smallish
haddock for breakfast.

At a quarter
to ten, he was feeling
very peculiar indeed.

And, at half past ten,
he wished he was dead.

"I feel seasick," he
said to his father.
"Vikings don't get seasick,"
said Stoick the Vast.

But this one was, all over Stoick's feet.
Hiccup got sicker and sicker . . .
and the storm got wilder and wilder.

Stoick the Vast sang the Viking Song at the storm.
But the storm took no notice.
A great wave came up and soaked him.

One mighty wave picked up that whole Viking ship as if it were a matchstick and threw it fifty miles to the south. And one mighty blast from the gale picked up that whole Viking ship as if it were a piece of seaweed and threw it fifty miles to the west.

And a terrible black wind went shrieking all over the lonely ocean and turned that Viking ship upside down and inside out and went shivering down every single Viking's spine.

"We're lost," said Stoick the Not-So-Vast-After-All. And a funny thing happened. His face began to turn a greenish hue, and he thought of the thirty-seven largish haddock he had had for breakfast . . . and his stomach began to heave.

And then all the Vikings turned a pretty green color, and all their stomachs heaved, and with an almighty rush they ran to the side . . .

"Well, well," said Hiccup. "It appears that Vikings DO get seasick."
And immediately he began to feel better.
"This direction!" shouted Hiccup.

But the Vikings were too busy
being seasick to steer the boat.
So Hiccup began to take charge.
And a funny thing happened.
The more he steered, the better he felt.

As he headed for home, that stormy wind filled the sails, and the boat skimmed over the ocean at one thousand miles an hour. Out of the depths of the sea came shoals of flying fish and leaping dolphins and strange whales with horns like unicorns.

There were eels that lit up like lightbulbs, and nameless things
with enormous eyes that no one had ever seen before—all
following Hiccup the Viking as he steered that ship at
tremendous speed toward home.

"Nice, breezy day," hummed Hiccup as he steered into the harbor.

"So tell me," said Old Wrinkly—and his old seashell eyes might have been twinkling—"do Vikings ever get frightened?"

"Sometimes they do," said Stoick the Vast.

"But they get over it," said Hiccup the Viking.
"That's what makes them so BRAVE."

Vikings ~~Never~~ Sometimes
get Seasick

The End

Little, Brown and Company

Hachette Book Group
237 Park Avenue, New York, NY 10017
Visit our website at lb-kids.com

Little, Brown and Company is a division of Hachette Book Group, Inc.
The Little, Brown name and logo are trademarks of Hachette Book Group, Inc.

The publisher is not responsible for websites (or their content) that are not owned by the publisher.

First U.S. Edition: May 2014
Originally published in paperback by Hodder Children's Books as *Hiccup: The Viking Who Was Seasick*.

978-0-316-28635-0

10 9 8 7 6 5 4 3 2 1

SC

Printed in China

The illustrations for this book were done in ink line and wash on SCPO Matt Art – 157gsm.
The text was set in Garamond, and the display type is Priska Serif.